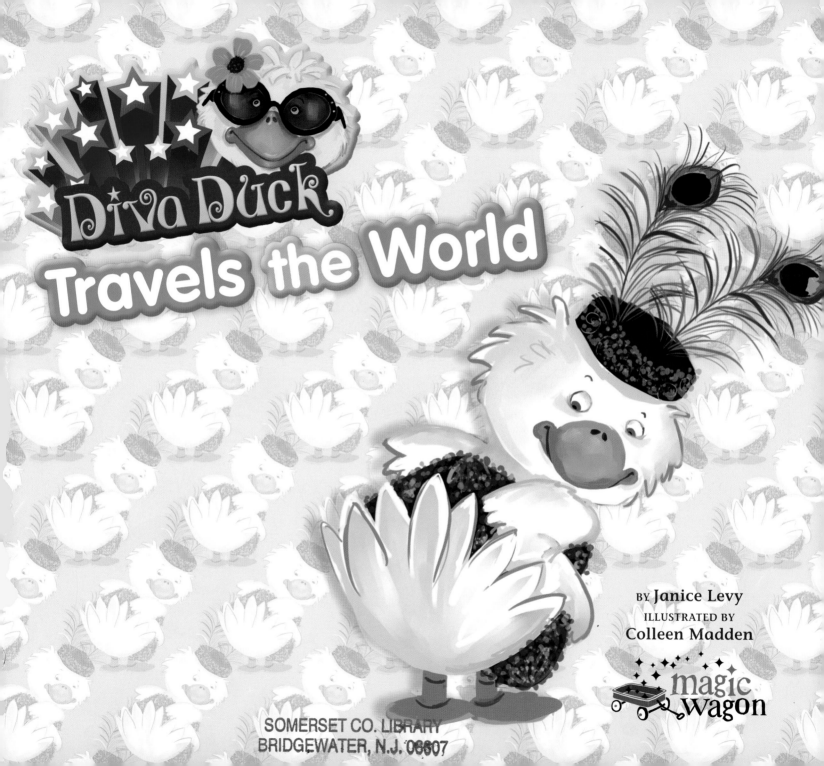

Diva Duck Travels the World

BY Janice Levy

ILLUSTRATED BY
Colleen Madden

magic Wagon

visit us at www.abdopublishing.com

Published by Magic Wagon, a division of the ABDO Group, PO Box 398166, Minneapolis, MN 55439. Copyright © 2013 by Abdo Consulting Group, Inc. International copyrights reserved in all countries. All rights reserved. No part of this book may be reproduced in any form without written permission from the publisher.

Looking Glass Library™ is a trademark and logo of Magic Wagon.

Printed in the United States of America, North Mankato, Minnesota.
052012
092012
This book contains at least 10% recycled materials.

Written by Janice Levy
Illustrations by Colleen Madden
Edited by Stephanie Hedlund and Rochelle Baltzer
Cover and interior design by Jaime Lint

Library of Congress Cataloging-in-Publication Data

Levy, Janice.
  Diva Duck travels the world / by Janice Levy ; illustrated by Colleen Madden.
      p. cm. – (Diva Duck)
    Summary: Diva Duck is famous and travels the world, but when disaster strikes the farm she finally remembers her friends.
    ISBN 978-1-61641-888-5
    1. Ducks–Juvenile fiction. 2. Animals–Juvenile fiction. 3. Friendship–Juvenile fiction. 4. Helping behavior–Juvenile fiction. 5. Fame–Juvenile fiction. (1. Ducks–Fiction. 2. Animals–Fiction. 3. Friendship–Fiction. 4. Helpfulness–Fiction. 5. Fame–Fiction.) I. Madden, Colleen M., ill. II. Title.
    PZ7.L5832Djt 2012
    (E)–dc23
                                        2011051964

Diva Duck traveled the world.

Her CD,
"Diva Fever,"
hit the top
of the charts.

Concert videos flooded the internet.

Her clothing line flew off the racks.

"I am Diva Duck, destined for greatness!" she quacked. Nothing could stop her. She was one hot duck.

At first, Diva was homesick.
She missed the friends she'd
left on the farm. She sang into her
cell phone. She waved from a Webcam.

Diva's friends
missed her, too. The farmer
decorated the barn with her postcards.

But, as days passed,
Diva got busier.

She **rapped** with rhinos and **strutted** with peacocks.

She **hip-hopped** with kangaroos.

Diva **danced** up pyramids and **deejayed** from the Great Wall of China.

"Diva Duck — Party Animal,"
read the headlines. The duck lived la vida loca.

Soon, Diva stopped writing letters.

WE ♥♥♥♥ ♥♥♥ DIVA

July 1, 2012
Dear Diva!
Hi!! How are you?
I'll bet Egypt is
so cool! I know u
must be so busy—
maybe too busy to
write back to us
on the farm? We

She turned off her cell phone.
She left her laptop behind.

Got a New TRACTOR
for Farmer Ted! We
saved up all of our
money that we made
at the fair. He was
so suprised but really
happy! Sheep says
Baa—Cow says Moo—
We miss you!
write back soon!
Don't forget us! ♥♥Pig

"I am Diva Duck, destined for greatness!" she shouted.

She made new friends and
forgot the "hood" for good.

Until one day, a terrible tornado hit the farm.

HELP-A-HELP-A-HELLLP!

The animals were in trouble!
The rooster crowed on the radio.

BAHHHH AHH!

The sheep bleated to the press.

The pigeons carried the news far and wide.

The animals booked the first flight out.
They knocked on Diva Duck's dressing room door.

"You **never** write, you **never** call," said the farmer.

"Do **we** need to make an appointment?"

"Make it quick," Diva said. "I've got records to spin."

"Speaking of spinning . . . ," said the farmer.

And then all the animals began to talk at once.

Diva's beak **twitched.**
Her hips **swiveled.**
Her tail went **boom-ducka-boom.**

"A duck's gotta do what a
duck's gotta do," she sighed.
"Let's go home."

Diva held a big concert.
She **flapped** her wings
and let it **fly**.

"Help the farm,
my little Quackers!"
she shouted.

Diva's fans
mopped and swept
and sawed and painted.

The animals moved back to the old neighborhood.

"Hip-hop hooray for Diva!" they cheered. "Rock on!"

"There's **no place like home**,"
said the farmer.

Diva **wiggled** her butt.

"And there's **no duck like me!**"

Diva Duck

★ Diva Duck traveled the world with her act. Where were some of the places they went?

★ Diva made many friends along the way and they came to help Diva's farm. How did they help?

★ Diva Duck went back to the farm to help her family after a disaster. What is one way you can help your community today?

About the Author: Janice Levy is the author of numerous award-winning children's books. Topics include bullying, multiculturalism, foster care, intergenerational relationships, and family values. She teaches creative writing at Hofstra University. Her adult fiction is widely published in magazines and anthologies.

About the Illustrator: Colleen Madden is an illustrator, mom, kickboxer, ukulele strummer, and honorary frog. She loves to draw for kids (and kids at heart!) and make people giggle. Diva Duck is her fourth series of children's books. She is currently writing her own titles as author/illustrator, which will all be very silly books.